This book is dedicated
to everyone I have had
the pleasure to work
with at Chilkat Guides

PRAISE FOR OTHER STORIES BY TOM LANG

coffee

". . . a deliciously satirical tale . . ."
        —*The Oregonian*
*"**coffee** romps through the highs and lows of the
Northwest's favorite rocket fuel with sardonic speed . . .
nimble, savory prose . . ."*
        —*The Register-Guard*
"A 'Days of Java and Roses' parody ... 59 hilarious pages."
        —*Willamette Week*
*"...an engaging story and it has literary merit. The book is
a little like espresso. It's small, tightly packed and full of
flavor ... as good as anything you find out of New York."*
        —*Doug Dutton, Dutton's Books, Los Angeles*

cat

*"Tom Lang's **cat** offers a deceptively deep and complex
story in the guise of a simple tale about a reformed cat
hater and his feline, Bouhaki. Lang paints his characters
with deft strokes, sweetly hooking his unsuspecting
reader's heart."*
        —*Shannon Brownlee, Senior Editor,
            U.S. News & World Report*

mrs. claus

*"... destined to become a holiday classic ... a painfully
funny story about the true meaning of giving and family."*
        —*Joe Kurmaskie, Author
            "Tales From Never-Never Land"*

eagle

A Story by
Tom Lang

Also by Tom Lang
coffee
cat
mrs. claus

Published by: BOUDELANG PRESS

P.O Box 3005

Venice, CA 90291-9998

TEL. 310.712.5606
WEBSITE: **www.boudelang.com**
E-mail BOUDELANG @aol.com

Illustration and concept by Andrew Reidenbaugh
Design by Siobhan Burns
Production by Nancy Phillips

Library of Congress Catalog Number 96-84755

ISBN 0-9649742-7-4

LIKE MOST SUB-ADULT MALES, I COULDN'T wait to mate, but, like, most sub-adult males, I did more waiting than mating. Just before my 5th birthday, when my head and tail turned as white as the Cathedral Peaks, I hit the eagle bars.

My first try was a wild roost in Skagway called the Gestation Station.   I auditioned, often but unsuccessfully, for the Mating Game, a weekly contest where a female with a blanket over her head chose from among a perch of male eagles after asking them silly questions.

My next stab was the Talon Lock, a bar down by the Haines airport. It wasn't much to look at—gravel on the floor, driftwood for stools, salmon skulls lying around the joint. And the Lock, as it was called, wasn't great for meeting females, either. The place could get rough. One night some ravens came in and me and the fellas had to stomp them.

Out of desperation I even joined a mating service called Soar and Score, but it turned out to be a multi-level marketing scam set up by eagles from California.

Then I discovered the Breed and Brood, a classy club located in the Council Grounds Complex, a thick stand of cottonwoods in the center of the Bald Eagle Preserve. The Brood had a contemporary debris decor—tin cans, Styrofoam cups, plastic bottles. The B & B was known to have the best entertainment in the valley, including a female a cappella group, the Aves Marias. A comedian was on limb the night I met Leu.

"What do you call an osprey living in a valley of eagles?" he asked the crowd.

"What?" an eagle chittered from the back.

"Hungry," said the comedian.

The crowd went cuckoo, flapping their wings, banging their tails on branches.

"Why did they want the turkey as the

national symbol instead of us?"

"I give up, why?" an eagle sitting up front said.

"Because turkeys are easier to shoot."

Flapping of wings, banging of tails.

Then Leu flew in and knocked me off my perch. She had big yellow eyes, nice plumage, sharp talons. She bounced over to the other side of my limb.

"Is this branch taken?" she asked sweetly.

"Uh...uh...uh...no," I said clumsily, a woodpecker attacking my heart.

"I'm Leu," she said.

"I'm Hal."

I was finishing the Brood's dinner special—spawned salmon tartar. The fish was aged to perfection with just a hint of early parasite infestation. She looked down at my

4

meal, held tightly between my talons.

"Did you know that a salmon has 79% eatable flesh, whereas a duck only has 68% eatable flesh?" she said.

"Well, no...I mean...yeah, I knew that."

Not only was she pretty, she was smart, too. She was raised in Juneau, she said, and she had just finished her studies as a coveted Stalmaster Scholar at the Raptor Center in Sitka. She pointed to objects a mile away and told me about the number of light sensitive cells, or photoreceptors, that determined the detail of vision for an eagle. We have 1 million per square millimeter of retina, she said, where tourists have 200,000.

Did I know, she asked, that our vision is 3 to 4 times greater than tourists and that we have both monocular and binocular visions? Or, that we perceive 5 basic colors, allowing us to see subtle tones and to pick out prey hiding in grass and brush?

I was mesmerized, molting at every word. We perched there for hours. The owner of the Brood finally interrupted us while Leu was explaining the different caloric counts between one hour of flapping and one hour of soaring and gliding (161 to 47).

"You two building a nest? We're closed. Scram."

I invited her down to the pier at Fort Seward in front of the little red building that used to be the telegraph office during the War Against the Eagles. We sat on the pilings and looked out at the water. A whale breeched in the middle of the Lynn Canal. I turned to her.

"Hungry? I'll go grab that sucker with my talons."

"Oh, stop," she said, placing her left wing over her bill to hide a giggle.

We talked and talked, opening up to each other. I confessed my fear of losing my feathers. She asked me if I thought she was fat. She felt she was putting on weight and had decided to consume less than 6 percent of her body weight each day as opposed to the average eagle's consumption of 7 to 12 percent of its body weight.

During a pause in our conversation, I gently preened her feathers and pecked at her bill. She lowered her head, spread her wings and let out a soft, high-pitched note.

"Nice vocal display," I said.

"Thank you very much."

For the next few weeks I chased her

through the sky. Talons touching, we practiced rolling together as we exchanged positions. Then, on a Thursday night at the Gestation Station, we won the Cartwheel Display when we performed a complicated, innovative dive highlighted by triple axle spins and whirls.

We talked about honeymooning in Glacier Bay, shopping for a nest site. Kids.

I FLEW DOWN TO THE ROOST TO SEE MY buddies. We exchanged the traditional eagle greeting.

"Ya all right?"

"Pretty good, ya all right?"

"I'm all right, uh huh, I'm okay."

The whole gang was there. Fovea Joe was originally from down south but he flew up one summer and decided to stay. Old

Man Canus, close to 40-years-old, was constantly picking up garbage and trying to find a use for it. Crazy Clo was, well, crazy as a loon. He suffered from Numerative Plumage Syndrome, an obsessive disorder where an eagle constantly counts his 7,182 feathers. Not much is known about NPS, but Leu told me they think the disease is triggered by stress. Rumor has it Clo began his downward spiral into feather counting after the love of his life flew south.

"Morning, Hal," Fovea Joe said,"you seem to be flying high today."

"Sure am," I said.

"2,162, 2,163, 2,164.." Clo counted off in his corner of the cottonwood.

"What gives Hal?" Canus said, working on a tin can he had found on the Haines Highway.

"Well, fellas, I've found a mate," I said proudly.

Canus looked up from his tin can. Clo stopped counting. Fovea Joe rubbed his beak.

"You mean mate as in nest, screaming eaglets 24-hours-a-day?" Fovea Joe said.

"As in mate FOR LIFE?" Canus said.

"Uh, yeah," I said.

"What do you know about her?"

"Well, she's smart, loving, considerate.."

"Hah!" Fovea Joe said,"that'll last one season, max."

"Million to one it'll work," Clo said.

"Have you met her mother?" Canus asked.

"Her mother?" I said, a thin layer of storm clouds forming in the back of my brain.

"Yes, her mother. Got to meet her mother. That's what she'll be in 5 years. Her mother's a vulture, you better catch the first thermal out of there."

"Seen it a thousand times," Clo said.

"You don't want to limit your choices, Hal," Fovea Joe said. "What if someone better comes along? Happened to a good friend of mine. Nothing he could do, being mated for life and all. Never see him."

"She sounds suspicious to me," Canus said, "a little too good to be true. I haven't even met her and I can tell you she has more problems than a raven has tricks."

"Never build a nest with someone who has more troubles than you," Fovea Joe said.

"You got that right," Canus said.

"Say good-bye to Thursday night at the

Gestation Station."

"So long to the Talon Lock."

"Bye-bye Breed and Brood."

"WAAAAAAAAAAH! WAAAAAAAAAAH!"

Leu and I were in our nest. Our two children, daughter Emma, son Juvie, were wailing for food. Leu, quite a bit heavier than when we first met, was stomping around.

"We need a fish every 3 hours for two chicks, Hal. Let's go!"

"Waaaaaaaah! Waaaaaaaah!"

"C'mon, Hal, if you can't handle this, what are you going to do when they're almost grown and need 2 pounds at each meal?"

I felt as if a trumpeter swan was stuck in my skull. There were strings attached to my wings pulling me far, far away.

"Aiiiiieeeeee!" I woke up screaming. I'd been snoozing on a cottonwood near where the Tsirku River feeds into the Chilkat. A raft full of tourists were taking my picture.

"DID YOU FORGET ABOUT OUR APPOINT-MENT?"

"Appointment?"

"Hello? The tree realtor is dropping by to show us some nest sites."

"Oh...right, right."

"Are you okay, Hal?"

"Me? Fine, Leu, great."

"Would you like to do a little

Cartwheel Display before we look at trees?"

"I'd love to, but, geez, you know, I have this headache that's killing me."

"Hal?"

"Yeeeeah?"

"What's going on?"

"Uh...nothing...I mean, not really...you know...everything's fine...sort of...not really, but you know...that's okay...everything's great."

"Hal?"

"Well...it's sort of...let me see...things seem to be moving kind of quickly...you know...and I thought...you being so smart and stuff...that you would think...a..."

"Think what, Hal?'

"Oh...you know, how fast things are going...how we really don't know each other that well...geez, I've never even met your mother..."

"We're not mating, is that what you're telling me?"

"Well, no. I mean yes. Not right now. But I still want to see you."

"Good-bye, Hal."

"You're not upset, are you Leu?"

"Why would I be upset, Hal, since I'm so smart. And stuff."

"I'll call you."

"Don't bother."

FOR THE NEXT TWO WEEKS I SPENT DAY and night in the bars, celebrating my freedom. However, something happened one night at the Gestation Station, while I was leading the crowd in a rousing rendition of "99 Tails of Trout on the Shore."

Between the 59th and 60th tail, a wave of stupidity and loss blew over me. I ruffled the feeling away. I was having too much fun.

Then at the Talon Lock, I started a driftwood clearing brawl when I clarified for the crowd a distinction that Leu had taught me— that the robin was actually the national bird whereas the bald eagle was the national symbol.

"What kind of carrion you trying to feed us, boy?" a big, burly eagle said to me.

"Yeah, what kind of dodo bird told you that one?" said another.

"She's no dodo bird, okay?" I said, heating up. "If there's any dodo birds around here, I'm looking at them."

Wings were flapped, beaks were exchanged, talons were locked.

Feathers flew.

And things weren't going so well at the Breed and Brood, either. I had carved in the gravel a detailed map to help explain Bergmann's Rule (members of warm-blooded species tend to be larger in the cooler parts of the breeding range, helping to preserve their body heat). My date stared at me and said,"Huh?"

I thought I was clicking with this one cutie so I invited her down to the pier to watch the whales.

"Hungry? I'll go grab one of those orcas for you."

"They're too big," she said. "I don't think you can lift it."

"4,442, 4,443, 4,444..."

"Afternoon, Hal," Fovea Joe said, "you seem to be flying kind of low today."

"I'm flying fine," I said defensively.

"Whatever."

"Not whatever, I'm flying fine," I said, my feathers ruffling slightly.

"4,661, 4,662, 4,663..." Clo droned on in the background.

"Whoa, time out," Fovea Joe said, walking over to me. "You can't scavenge a scavenger, Hal. What's the problem?"

"You got that right," Canus said, playing with a bread bag he had picked up from a tourist luncheon, "you can't scavenge a scavenger."

"5,001, 5,002, 5,003..."

"Still miss that female, huh?" Fovea Joe said.

"Yeah, I suppose."

"It'll pass. Come on, hang out with us for awhile. We'll cheer you up."

I looked over at Clo.

"5,298, 5,299, 5,300..."

I looked over at Canus. He was dragging a piece of webbing from the river. I turned to Fovea Joe.

"I don't think so."

I took off down the Chilkat Valley, caught a thermal, dipped over the range into Chilkoot Lake, flew down to Haines and back up the Chilkat River. I spied a salmon, a 3-pounder or so, working his way up a thin channel near where the Tsirku River meets the Chilkat. I dove, leveled off near the water and snatched the salmon right at the tail. Yes, perfect, I thought as I lifted off. However, the salmon tossed and turned and just as I gained momentum, I lost my grip and the fish tumbled to the water, disappearing in the deeper channel.

I was losing my touch.

I KNEW I'D FIND LEU DOWN ON THE LOWER delta of the Tsirku conducting one of her science experiments. I landed beside her.

"Hello, Leu."

"Hello," she said, her tone an icy wind blowing out of Skagway.

"What ya doing?"

"Counting. I'm disturbed by the

disproportion of sockeye coming back to spawn and the corresponding smolt going out to sea."

"Hmmm, fascinating," I said.

We sat in silence while she worked. I drummed a talon on a tree trunk that had washed up on the gravel bar.

"Ah...I've been thinking, Leu...uh...I think I'm ready to mate."

"Really?"

"Really."

"Have you found a victim yet?"

"Very funny," I said. "I thought, you know, we could try it again."

"Well, you're thinking, Hal, and that's good. But you're thinking wrong, and that's bad."

Some type of sea eagle landed between us. Leu perked up.

"I'm sorry I'm late, Leu-Leu," the eagle said with a regional accent I wasn't familiar with. He pecked her on both sides of the face. "Just the thought of seeing you wreaks havoc with my regulated heterothermy, fluctuating my body temperature way beyond the narrow range of an eagle."

"Oh, Aquilo," Leu said, giggling.

Aquilo?

"Leu-Leu," he continued, "the cones and rods of your beautiful yellow eyes illuminate me and bring depth and perception to my life."

"Oh, Aquilo," Leu said again.

"Excuse me," I said, hacking a few times, "must be some DDT residue drifting up from down south, because it's getting pretty thick around here."

They ignored me. I lifted off, an invisible log dragging my heart down into the river.

"Leu-Leu, I know they say that male and female eagle plumages are the same, but there are those of us who are monomorphic, then there is you. Nature pays homage to your plumage; rivers choke with spawning salmon and lakes overflow with baby ducks."

"Oh, Aquilo."

I WASN'T HAPPY. AND IF I WASN'T HAPPY, nobody was going to be happy.

I came up behind an arctic tern and whacked him with a body slam. I swooped down and scattered a couple of crows snacking on a fish on a gravel bar. Flying over a raft full of tourists, I posed for their photos, then I laid some droppings on them.

Down by where the Chilkat flows into the Lynn Canal a sea otter was swimming on its back, a little baby trout in its paws. Doubling behind the otter's head so he couldn't see me, I dropped down behind him, skimmed across the water and snatched the fish out of his hands.

"Hey!" the otter yelled at me, "you stole my fish!"

I circled above him, the fish flopping back and forth in my talons.

"Give me back my fish, you kleptoparasite!" he fussed, slapping the water.

"Such language," I said calmly, circling lower, dangling the fish just out of his reach.

"GIVE ME BACK MY FISH, YOU OVERRATED, SCAVENGING VULTURE!"

"I'd love to stay but I'm starving."

I leaned to the right, caught the wind

and headed up river, the otter's curses
fading in the distance.

EAGLES DON'T JUST STEAL FROM OTHER animals. We rob from each other, as well. We don't advertise the fact since we are the national symbol and all.

However, the word "stealing" was never uttered in our nest while I was growing up. My mother called it "displacement."

"Crows steal, ravens steal," she would say while she ripped bits of flesh from a flopping salmon. "We displace."

Right, Mom.

This is how it works. An eagle catches a fish and starts to eat it. Eagles land nearby, waiting for an opportunity to "displace" him. One eagle will take the initiative and flap, shove, beak, or talon wrestle the first eagle out of the way. Well, it wasn't going to happen today.

Two big, dumb Yukon eagles landed near me while I ate my little trout.

"Hey, Waldo, what say we have us a bite to eat?"

"I could stand a kilogram or two, Dorp."

I looked over at them and stopped eating. I covered the food with my wings.

"Listen up, my mentally challenged falconiformes. I am going to talk *reeeeeal* slow so you don't have a problem understanding. You make one move toward my lunch and I will pull your third eyelid down over your bill, then I will carve tic-tac-toe on your throat with my talons. Are our voices on the same frequency?"

The two Canadian eagles looked at each other.

"Eh, we're eagles. We steal from each other. You trying to mess with nature?"

"No, dumbos, nature's trying to mess with me. Scram, go home."

I flapped my wings at them and they took flight, bumped into each other, then flew in circles. They landed back in the same spot. I gave them the stink eye.

"Uh, sorry, but, uh, eh, which way is north?"

"HOW DO YOU SAVE A BOATLOAD OF drowning pesticide salesmen?"

"HOW?" the eagle crowd crowed.

"Who cares?"

The Breed and Brood audience let out a collective "ooooooh" followed by laughter.

"What do you call two Spotted Owls in the same forest?"

"WHAT?"

"History."

Wings flapped and tails banged.

I was sitting on a branch at the Brood, one wing draped over a twig. I was cocky from anger and rejection. A pretty female, quite a bit larger than me, landed close by.

"Nice wing primaries," I said.

"Flap off," she said, not even looking at me.

"What's your problem, hon? You wake up on the endangered list?"

"I'm not your hon," she said, turning her neck 270 degrees to face me. Her feathers went back. "Hal? Is that you? It's me, Cece, your third cousin, fourth time removed. Stop flirting with me. You look awful. Get some help."

An immature female landed on a limb above me. A pretty girl, she couldn't have been more than 4-years-old. Her eyes were still creamy, her beak gray and yellow, her head gray and light brown, her lower breast brown with some gray, her wing tips mottling gray, her tail gray with black.

"Buy me a salmon?" she said, trying to be sexy.

"How old are you?"

"Uh...er...uh...five," she said.

"I don't think so, hon. If you were five, your eyes and beak would be yellow, your wings all brown and your head and tail white."

"Ah..er...I dye them to make myself look younger."

"You should be home with your parents."

"Well, pops, I guess if you had a mate, you'd be home with her, now wouldn't you?"

The image of Leu and Aquilo cut across my field of vision like a chainsaw. The immature female flittered to another branch. An eagle from a few limbs over spoke up.

"Hey, pal, why don't you leave the ladies alone, okay?"

"And, ah, who would be making me leave the ladies alone...pal?"

"Me," the eagle said, pushing his chest out.

"You and what flock?"

Two of the Brood's bouncers pinned my wings back, dragged me outside and roughed me up.

"And stay out, pal," they said as they shoved me into a gravel bar.

"THEY MURDERED YOUR GREAT GRAND-father right here in the Chilkat Valley; gunned him down in front of his wife and two children."

"Yes, Grandpa."

"He was in the prime of his life, only 12-years-old."

"Yes, Grandpa."

"It was a bad time to be an eagle back

47

then. We call it the Massacre, the Reign of Terror. They slaughtered 100,000 of us over a 35-year span. Wiped out entire families."

"Yes, Grandpa." There was good news and bad news back then...

"There was good news and bad news back then, boy. Good news was the rivers were packed with spawned out, dead, decaying salmon; the bad news was we were all dead and decaying, too."

Grandpa chuckled and coughed up a pellet or two. I waited patiently.

"Bad news was we were all dead and decaying, too," Grandpa repeated, jettisoning another pellet across the nest.

"Yes, Grandpa."

"So," my grandfather said after a long silence, "you're having some female problems, are you?"

"Uh, yes."

"And you've come by to visit your old grandfather for some sage advice. Am I correct?"

"Correct."

"Well, my boy," Grandpa said, putting an old, battered wing over mine, "I can't help you. I haven't a clue."

My bill dropped open. I tried to say something.

"You know, the killings stopped way before you were hatched...the Feds didn't always protect us...you kids take the Preserve for granted...I remember the first..."

"GET THIS THING OFF ME!"

Canus was wrapped up in a fish net he had dragged from the river. Fovea Joe, Clo and I slowly untangled the mess. Canus shook his feathers.

"You should stick to bread bags," I said.

"Hrmmmph," Canus said.

"6,101, 6,102, 6,103..."

"We warned you about being involved

in this mating game, Hal," Fovea Joe said.

"Warned you a million times," Clo said, "...6,222, 6,223..."

"Watch out for her mother, I told you," Canus said.

"Wait, fellas, I need advice on how to get her back, not on how to stay away from her."

The gang sat there, no expression, staring out at the river.

"You know," I said, "now that I think about it, have any of you ever been mated?"

"Of course I have," Fovea Joe said, "...well, not really...sort of...what's your point?"

"Yeah, what are you getting at?" Canus said. "If I wanted to be mated, females would be lined up and down the Chilkat. It would look like the largest congregation of eagles in the world."

"Thousands," Clo said.

"Right, fellas," I said, "and I have a nest in a clear-cut to sell you."

I FLEW UP THE TSIRKU, CROSSED OVER TO THE Klehini, flapped all the way down the Chilkat past Davidson and Rainbow glaciers, then across Mud Bay and back through Haines.

Then it hit me. I would build a nest. I found a tall spruce on the banks of the Tsirku near the inlet to Chilkat Lake where the sockeyes go to spawn. Crazed like a magpie, I hauled twigs, moss and debris to my building site. In 3 to 4 days I had built a nest that looked like an ad for the Forest of Dreams.

I was putting some finishing touches on the place—moss in the center, fireweed around the outside—when I heard the flap of wings above me. It was Leu.

"Good location, Hal. Nice tall tree. Serves as a superb observation post and acts as a signal to unwanted visitors. The height also provides unobstructed flight paths for us as eagles since we have a problem becoming airborne and maneuvering in dense foliage."

"Duuuuh," I said.

We sat in silence while I nodded my head up and down.

"Hungry?" I said, looking around the

nest. "I know I've got something laying around."

"No, I'm stuffed. I stole a sockeye from a couple of Canadian eagles on my way over."

"Where's Aquilo?" I asked, the name sticking in my craw.

"Oh, Aquilo has gone back south. We had some species and genus issues."

"Hmmmm."

"And I have to get back to work," Leu said, flapping her wings.

"Wait, Leu. Why don't you tuck your wings back and stay a while? We could preen a little, maybe do some light talon locking. Like old times. What do you say?"

"Old times give me a headache, Hal."

"But these are new times."

"Not yet, Hal. I'll call you."

Leu dropped out of the nest and flapped her wings. A feather from her breast fluttered in the wind and landed on the nest. I gently picked the feather up with my bill and placed it in the center of the twigs. I sat and admired it. One, I said to myself as I started to laugh. Only 7,181 more to go.

AUTHOR'S NOTES

The Bald Eagle is of the genus Haliaeetus (hals, Greek for sea, and aetos, eagle) and the species leucocehalus (white-headed). The sub-species of the northern Bald Eagle is alascanus.

The fovea is a cup-like depression in the retina, home for a high concentration of sensory cells.

Between 1917 and 1952, Alaska offered a 50-cent to $2 bounty on the Bald Eagle. More than 100,000 eagles were shot and killed.

BOUDELANG PRESS ORDER FORM

NAME_____

STREET_____

CITY_____STATE_____ZIP_____

Add $1 for shipping on individual book orders. For 3 or more books, add a flat $3.

	mrs. claus			TOTAL
Quantity	_____		x $7=	_____
Coffee	cat	eagle		
_____	____	____	x $5=	_____
salmon	bear			
_____	____		x $5=	_____
Shipping			+	_____
			TOTAL DUE =	_____

__ **MASTERCARD** __ **VISA** __ **CHECK**

CARD #_____

EXP. DATE_____

PRINT NAME AS SHOWN ON CARD

_____

Please make checks payable to:

    BOUDELANG PRESS

    P.O Box 3005, Venice, CA 90291-9998

Questions? Please call 310.712.5606 or e-mail us at BOUDELANG@aol.com. Please visit our website www.boudelang.com.